The Essential Guide

Written by Brian J. Bromberg

Contents

Pabl

Uniqua

Tyrone

Tasha

Austin

The Backyard!

Get ready for adventures as big as your imagination with The Backyardigans! Each day, Pablo, Tyrone, Uniqua, Tasha, and Austin get together to explore the whole wide world without ever leaving the backyard!

Pablo's House

Adventure Begins

Each adventure begins and ends in the backyard. The Backyardigans may travel to the Wild West, the Deep Jungle, or outer space, but when the adventures end, they never need to travel far for a snack!

Five Fantastic Friends

Pablo the penguin, Tyrone the moose, and Uniqua the ... well, Uniqua ... are neighbors who share a backyard. They often invite over their friends Tasha the hippo and Austin the kangaroo to join their imaginary journeys!

Tyrone's House

Uniqua's House

Imagine the Possibilities!

When the Backyardigans use their imagination, they can turn their sandbox into a desert island, their kiddie pool into an ocean, their slide into a castle turret, or their picnic table into a rocket ship!

Pablo

Pablo is an energetic little penguin who thinks, speaks, acts, and reacts quickly. But he's no birdbrain. His friends can always count on him to come up with big, exciting backyard adventures.

Backyard Buddies

Pablo's house shares its backyard with Tyrone and Uniqua's houses, so he's never far from an adventure with his best friends. And the color of Pablo's house matches his color!

Pablo always wears his blue bowtie!

Movin' and Groovin'

Pablo is not very graceful, but he sure can dance, whether it's a groovy solo or whether he's movin' to the music with all his friends!

Pablo's propeller
beanie is his
favorite hat!

Playful Penguin

Pablo loves to share surprises with his friends. Sneaking up on Tyrone and Uniqua is one of his surprise specialties!

The Perfect Pair

Pablo imagines lots of thrilling adventures, but if his imagination runs away with him, he knows he can always count on his best friend Tyrone to help him overcome anything!

Pablo, Calm Down!

Pablo is a bit tightly wound, so sometimes a challenge might make him run in a circle, flap his flippers up and down, and FREAK OUT! Luckily, his friends are always around to calm him down!

Pablo As...

Pablo swings into all kinds of imaginary adventures with his friends! He takes the lead on many of their missions, but other times, he's just as eager to follow the leader. He's been ...

An Expert Tracker

Cowboy Pablo rides the range on his trusty horse, confident that he can pick up the trail of the thieving bandit that Cowgirls Uniqua and Tasha aim to find.

Different adventures sometimes call for different hats—like a pirate hat!

Pablo Plays

Viking Pablo sets sail with his crew to find a land that no one has ever discovered before.

Surfer Pablo sets out in his rad dune buggy to find Tiki Beach so he can surf the perfect wave.

Pie-ya! Ninja Pablo leads a raid on the Imperial Palace to get a taste of the Great Pie.

Super Villain

Wa-ha-ha! As Yucky Man, Super Villain Pablo tries to take over the world!

"A pirate says, "ARRR!" Try it!"

The World's Greatest Detective

Who can figure out who took Lady Tasha's jewels at Mystery Manor? Elementary! The World's Greatest Detective, Pablo! He'll discover who's behind this mystery!

Uniqua

Daring, dancing Uniqua is totally unique. She's graceful, agile, and light on her feet, but when it comes to playing, she's more "adventure" than "ballet." Try to keep up with her!

Uniqua's antennae help make her quite unique indeed!

Pretty in Pink

She may look like a pink little cutie-pie, but Uniqua loves adventure and action. She's got a can-do attitude and she won't let any quest get the best of her!

Adventure Calls

Uniqua often comes up with exciting quests for her friends. When she reads them the legend of the Flying Rock at StoneStep Hill, they all decide to go searching for it!

Brave... and Brilliant

Professor Uniqua, brilliant scientist, isn't afraid of jungle perils! She confidently leads the way into the Deep Jungle … even though Jungle Heroes Pablo, Tyrone, and Austin are the ones that live there!

"Hi, I'm Uniqua! Let's dance!"

A Good Friend

Uniqua is very sweet—she knows whether her friends are happy or sad, and she'll always say something to show she cares. Even while lost in space, Commander Uniqua has time to cheer up a friend.

Just for Laughs

Besides running, climbing, and adventuring, Uniqua has a knack for being silly. She likes to:

✳ Tell silly jokes

✳ Make mysterious noises

✳ Sneak up on her friends for "tickle time!"

Uniqua As...

Uniqua is always ready to help her friends explore the four corners of the earth (and beyond) ... and all without ever leaving the backyard! She's set sail into adventure as ...

If you want to explore the rainforest, you'd better bring an umbrella!

Captain Uniqua

ARRRR you ready for high-seas adventure with Captain Uniqua? She leads her pirate crew in search of treasure ... and tries to get to it before Captain Pablo!

Uniqua Underhood

On this "whodunnit" mystery, Uniqua surprises her friends by revealing that she's a police officer from London who has come to stop a crime.

Uniqua the Pink

Uniqua the Pink goes on a quest to deliver Queen Tasha's message to King Austin, overcoming challenges along the way to become a brave knight.

Professor Uniqua

She may be a brilliant scientist, but even brilliant scientists can get stuck in the muck sometimes—especially if that muck is quicksand!

"I'm Professor Uniqua, the brilliant scientist!"

Sphinx Uniqua

In Ancient Egypt, Sphinx Uniqua teaches Princess CleoTasha the secret of the Nile—saying "please" and "thank you!"

Ski Patroller Uniqua

The Ski Patrol is in control when Uniqua hits the slopes to save her friends—even if they don't need saving at all!

Tyrone

Tyrone is the nicest little moose you ever met. He's an easygoing, laid-back kid with a relaxed attitude, a sunny smile, and a cool head (of antlers) on his shoulders.

"Hi! I'm Tyrone."

You can always see Tyrone's antlers, even when he's wearing a hat!

Best Friends

Each day, Pablo knows that he can count on his neighbor and best friend Tyrone to join him on his imaginary adventures ... wherever they may lead!

One Confident Moose

Tyrone is a confident kid—he enjoys figuring out how to overcome challenges and solve problems!

Sherman the Worman

Sherman is not a just worm; he's a Worman who speaks Worman-ese. Tyrone understands him and helps him on adventures, whether hitting the trail to Wyoming or finding his home deep in the jungle!

Stuck in the Middle

Tyrone is a very calm kid, so he often finds that it's his job to cool down his hot-tempered friends like Uniqua and Tasha. Lucky for them, Tyrone can always help to chill them out.

"This is certainly an icy adventure!"

Tyrone is always ready to slide into adventure!

Count on Me

Tyrone may seem a little slower than his speedy buddy, Pablo, but they're a perfect match. Whatever problem Pablo imagines, Tyrone can help him solve.

Tyrone As...

From a Mountie on duty to a deep-sea diver to a mysterious Swamp Creature, Tyrone has played many roles. Each day in the backyard is a chance to see just how far this moose's imagination can take him!

Surfer Dude

Surf's up! Surfer Tyrone is the moose with the moves— totally rad moves that help him to find and ride the perfect wave with his friends at Tiki Beach. Ho, daddy!

Captain Tyrone

Yep, he's a pirate captain too! Aboard this ship, all the pirates can be captains, as long as they can sing a pirate song, do a pirate dance, search for pirate treasure, and of course, say ARRRR!

"I'm Jungle Explorer Tyrone. I can talk to animals!"

Secret Agent

Shh! Secret Agent Tyrone helps his friends to sneak past a Treasure Museum's booby traps to return missing treasure to its owner.

Mysterious Butler

Whether he's Butler Tyrone, a detective searching for monsters, or even a ghost, Tyrone knows what to do in a mysterious mansion: be very quiet and listen!

Jungle Explorer Tyrone gets into the swing of things!

Mission Controller

The astronauts can rest easy knowing that Tyrone is in control at Mission Control!

Tasha

Don't be fooled. Tasha may look sweet as pie, but she's a my-way-or-the-highway kind of hippo who can be a tad bit bossy. Still, she can also be just as giggly and playful as any of her backyard friends.

Smile!

It's easy for Tasha to smile when she comes over to play with her best friend, Uniqua. She loves posing for the camera and being the center of attention!

Tasha's red mary janes

Snow Way!

Tasha is determined, headstrong, highly motivated to get her own way ... well, okay, she's stubborn. When she plays the Frozen North expert, you'd better take her expert advice.

"Hi, I'm Tasha!"

Tasha has Arrived

Tasha loves to play with her friends, especially when she can be the queen while her friends play her loyal subjects!

Make Way for Royalty!

Tasha loves being a princess, so much that she'll sing a song about it. And when Tasha sings, this diva deserves to be the center of attention.

Tasha As...

Tasha really knows how to get into the act in style. When she comes over to play, she brings her big personality with her (and a little attitude too). She's been ...

Ravishing Royalty

Tasha loves being in charge, so it makes sense that she's up for any adventure where she's a princess, a medieval queen, the ruler of Ancient Egypt, or the Empress of feudal Japan!

Mermaid Tasha

Tasha has her own way of playing along. When her friends the Vikings try to discover a new land, she tries to stop them and make them sing her song.

Brilliant Scientist Tasha

Inspired by the brilliant scientist Uniqua, Tasha sets out to be an even *more* brilliant scientist!

"I'm Ski Patroller Tasha! Ski Patrol to the rescue!"

As a member of the Ski Patrol, Tasha always keeps hot cocoa ready for her rescues!

Mad Scientist

Tasha sends Assistant Austin on a mission so she can plan her maddest creation yet—a surprise birthday party for him!

Tasha helps

Tasha doesn't always have to be the center of attention. Sometimes, she helps her friends as:

Mission Controller: The astronauts couldn't have made it to Mars without her!

Lady Tasha: When her jewels were stolen ... okay, maybe she does always need to be the center of attention!

Austin

Austin is sweet, earnest, and always ready to bounce into any backyard game. He's the new kangaroo on the block, and a little slow to take the lead, but expect the unexpected when he comes over to play.

Eager Austin

Austin gets an extra-special spring in his step from being included in his friends' backyard adventures, and he's always eager to get involved!

A Kangaroo of Few Words

Austin is a quiet kid who can be a little shy and perhaps hesitant to share his ideas. In fact, as a Jungle Hero, he only says one word: "Ugh!"

Rover

Austin always brings a new twist to every adventure. On a mission to Mars, Astronaut Austin has an incredible companion named Rover, a lunar robot that acts like a dog!

22

Austin loves to play! He can usually be seen with a big smile!

King for a Day

Austin usually plays an assistant, a servant, or a crew member, but he plays important roles too—like a wise old emperor or a king in medieval times.

Austin and Friends

Austin's friends like doing things to show him that he's an important part of the group—like when they surprised him with a birthday party while they were playing monsters!

23

Austin As...

From an astronaut in outer space to a superhero protecting the world from evil-doers, Austin has played some awesome roles. He's been ...

"Mountie Austin reporting for duty"

Apprentice Austin

Apprentice Austin learns from Master Pie Maker Tyrone how to make the Great Pie—and how to defend it from pie-stealing ninjas.

Astronaut Austin

Astronaut Austin suits up for a mission to Mars. As Equipment Specialist, he's in charge of the high-tech stuff.

Racer Austin

Racer Austin has never won a gold medal before, but with his trusty racing pack, he speeds over land, sand, sea, and snow to win the big race around the world!

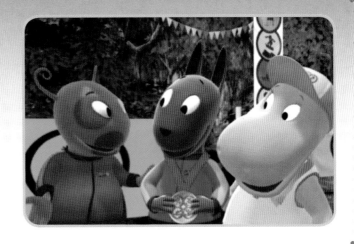

Mystery Lifeguard

Mystery Lifeguard Austin makes sure that all surfers seeking Tiki Beach first learn all the righteously rad moves they need to know!

Mountie Austin keeps the Yukon safe from Snow Fort raiders.

Captain Hammer

As Captain Hammer, Austin can build anything to help him stop evil-doers from capturing the Key to the World at the Tower of Power.

Mr. Frothingslosh

When Austin latches on to a phrase, he REALLY uses it. As Mr. Frothingslosh, one of the suspects at Mystery Manor, he often repeats the phrase "Great Caesar's Ghost!"

Frozen North

Mounties Pablo and Tyrone guard the World's Largest Snowball in their Snow Fort.

The Backyardigans love to explore the Frozen North—whether it's to find a legendary Yeti (Pablo), to throw a prehistoric cave party, to guard the world's largest snowball, or to discover the Secret of Snow!

Let's Get Going!

Frozen North explorers Tyrone, Uniqua, and Tasha need to make a run for it when a giant snowball comes rolling after them!

"Yeti-yeti-yeti-yeti!"

A Very Yeti Surprise!

The Frozen North Experts finally find their Yeti, and they find out his favorite thing too—to give snow-bellies to his friends!

Deep Jungle

Whether they're heading to the Heart of the Jungle, trying to find a Flying Rock, or running a worldwide race, the Backyardigans love to swing into Deep Jungle adventure!

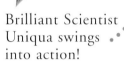

Brilliant Scientist Uniqua swings into action!

Jungle Experts

There's no time for hanging around when Explorers Uniqua and Tasha take a shortcut through the jungle to find the Flying Rock. But the tangled twosome don't have much choice!

Jungle Perils

Even Jungle Heroes Pablo, Tyrone, and Austin need to watch out for jungle perils—like an attack from the dreaded Can't-See-Ems! Careful! You can't see 'em!

Pirate Ship

Captains Uniqua and Austin sail the high seas in search of treasure. Will they find it before Captains Pablo and Tyrone, or will they walk the plank?

Musical Marauders

It's a pirate raid set to reggae when Captains Pablo and Tyrone storm Captain Uniqua's ship to keep her from reaching Treasure Island first!

"This is a VERY piratey adventure!"

Captain Austin has a hook for a hand!

Walk the Plank

Uniqua and Austin are forced to walk the plank ... but when Pablo and Tyrone see how exciting it looks, they want to walk the plank too. And everyone lands on Treasure Island!

The Map

Each pirate team has half a map. When they work together, they can put the map together and find the buried treasure!

Mission to Mars

The Backyardigans plot a course for far-out adventure!

It's an out-of-this-world adventure when intrepid Astronauts Uniqua, Pablo, and Austin blast off to Mars to discover the source of a strange signal being transmitted to Tyrone and Tasha at Mission Control!

Ready for Anything!

These astronauts aren't just hanging out! Commander Uniqua, Science Officer Pablo, and Equipment Specialist Austin are brave astronauts on a mission to the Red Planet!

Martian City

After braving a meteor shower and Martian caves, the crew makes it to an underground Martian City.

"Boinga! Boinga! Boinga!"

Long Distance Call

The astronauts discover the source of the signal is a little Martian phoning Mission Control to say "Boinga!" In Martian, that means "hello" (and everything else too).

Let's Dance

The Backyardigans sing and dance to a different style of music on each backyard adventure. Ancient Egypt rings out with Broadway-style show tunes, the superheroes and super villains dance to salsa, funk fills the Frozen North, and much more!

The friends take turns leading the singing and dancing!

Secret Agent Limbo

Tango music propels Secret Agents Pablo, Tyrone, and Uniqua through the secret passageways and booby traps of the Treasure Museum. Get in the groove as they limbo under the laser-beam security!

Ghosts with the Most

Ghosts Pablo, Tyrone and Uniqua show off some otherworldly moves, dancing and singing to 1920's-style jazz.

"Your backyard friends, the Backyardigans!"

A Space Age Dance

Kenyan High Life music backs the brave astronauts' mission to Mars. When they finally find the Martians, they celebrate with an out-of-this-world dance finale!

Mixed-up Music

Sometimes, unexpected music plays during each story. For example:

✳ In the Wild West, the cowboys and cowgirls dance to hip hop.

✳ Samurais and ninjas sing and dance to Spaghetti Western music.

EDITOR Amy Junor   SENIOR DESIGNER Jill Clark
CATEGORY PUBLISHER Alex Allan   DESIGNER Mika Kean-Hammerson
DTP DESIGNER Hanna Ländin   BRAND MANAGER Rob Perry
PRODUCTION Vivianne Ridgeway   PUBLISHING MANAGER Simon Beecroft

First published in the United States in 2007
by DK Publishing
375 Hudson Street
New York, New York 10014

07 08 09 10 11 10 9 8 7 6 5 4 3 2 1
BD319 - 10/06

DK books are available at special discounts for bulk purchases for
sales promotions, premiums, fund-raising, or educational use.
For details, contact: DK Publishing Special Markets, 375 Hudson Street, New York, NY 10014
SpecialSales@dk.com

A catalog record for this book is available from the Library of Congress.

ISBN: 978-0-7566-2703-4

Printed and bound in China by Hung Hing Printing

www.nickjr.co.uk
www.nickelodeon.com

Discover more at
www.dk.com